# RUDOLPH'S
# NOSE KNOWS

WRITTEN BY
MARCIA FISHMAN

ILLUSTRATED BY
STEVEN KATZ

RUDOLPH'S NOSE KNOWS
Written by Marcia Fishman
Illustrated by Steven Katz

Copyright © 2010 LIMEADE Publishing House
Registration Number TXu 1-669-843

Distributed by Operation Outreach-USA Press
Holliston, Massachusetts

ISBN 978-0-615-37839-8

Printed in the United States of America

# KINDNESS

is the language
which the deaf can hear
and the blind can see.

-Mark Twain

Upon a time not long ago
A dachshund came to fame.
And like a reindeer we all know,
Rudolph was his name.

Born blind and deaf, he could not watch
The dogs run in the park.
He'd try to raise his ears a notch
But could not hear them bark.

Though he was cute, he acted odd.
He'd stumble through the day.
The other dogs would call him "clod"
And all refused to play.

But then one night as black as coal,
A bird began to cry:
"My chick fell down a deep dark hole
And he's too young to fly!"

At dawn a dog yelled "Listen up!
A rescue is our quest.
But don't include the Rudolph pup.
He'll only be a pest."

The park dogs ran to gather 'round
To plan how they could help.
But even with their skills as hounds,
They cried a failing yelp.

The dogs had faced a major fact;
A flaw they couldn't control.
No matter how they tried to act,
They couldn't get down that hole.

The Newfoundland could save the chick
If he were found at sea.
The greyhound's speed was oh so quick,
But she couldn't set him free.

The collie knew that she could herd
A chick that went astray.
And if the pointer saw the bird,
He'd surely point the way.

"Who could help this little bird?"
Not one could pull this off.
But then, as if the dachshund heard,
Appeared the young Rudolph.

He stuck his nose down in the hole
And then began to crawl.
He burrowed like an expert mole
And found the chick, so small.

He told the chick, "Do not despair!
I know it's dark as night.
But I can travel anywhere
Without the use of light."

Rudolph used his nose to find
The opening in the dirt.
And even though the dog was blind,
They both emerged unhurt.

The mother bird lost all her fears.
Rudolph saved her son.
And though he could not hear the cheers
The revelry was fun.

The teasing stopped, there's love instead.
The dogs now play with pride.
And though Rudolph still bumps his head,
His nose is now his guide.

THE END

HOORAY FOR RUDOLPH!

# WORD FIND

Find these words:

**TEASE   LOVE   PRIDE   PLAY   CLOD**
**BLIND   DEAF   HELP   CHEER   FEAR**

Can you also find these words in the book:

T X W P H E L P
E K M R C L O D
A B L I N D B F
S Q Z D L O V E
E C H E E R I A
P L A Y R J Q R
U D E A F W J Z

(they will be in any straight line, either frontwards or up & down)

# MAKE A POEM

Can you complete the rhymes to make your own story?
Use the pictures to help.

## RUDOLPH'S FUNNY FRIENDS

Rudolph is a little dog
With friends as silly as the _____
Who sings while sitting on a log.

Another pal, a handsome fox
Parades around in fluffy socks
And loves to snuggle in a _____.

His friend the bird, with feathers red
Must fly up high to find her bed
With twigs as pillows for her _____.

Rudolph also knows a cat
Who wears a flower in her _____
While running fast to chase the rat.

Answers: frog, box, head, hat

# IMAGE FIND

## Can you find Rudolph and his friends?

(hint: there are seven hidden animals to find)

# Help Rudolph find the chick.

## About Operation Outreach–USA

Operation Outreach–USA (OO-USA) provides free literacy and character education programs to elementary and middle schools across the country.

Because reading is the gateway to success, leveling the learning field for at-risk children is critical. By giving books to students to own, confidence is built and motivated readers are created. OO-USA selects books with messages that teach compassion, respect and determination. OO-USA involves the school and the home with tools for teachers and parents to nurture and guide children as they learn and grow.

More than one million children in schools in all fifty states have participated in the program thanks to the support of a broad alliance of corporate, foundation and individual sponsors.

To learn more about Operation Outreach–USA and how to help, visit www.oousa.org, call 1-800-243-7929, or email info@oousa.org.